PRAISE FOR
THAT'S WHAT DADS ARE MADE FOR

As a child, I tried very hard to find positive things about my father. No dad is perfect, but each has positive qualities we can embrace. This is really important for kids to understand, especially in a social media driven world where we are prone to compare our lives to those of others. I think *That's What Dads Are Made For* will help kids to see what is unique and special in their relationships with their dads.

—Jen Miller, Executive Director of The Midland Center

Such a fun and simple way to express an indescribable love linking a child and father. While the relationship between a child and father is narrated from the viewpoint of a young one, it still tugs at the heart of a grown daughter who misses that relationship with her own father. Life is about moments, and moments form everlasting memories. *That's What Dads Are Made For* will do just that!

—Mandy McGeehan, Daughter, Mother, Avid Book Lover, and Teacher

Dad's relationships with their kids matter deeply. Amanda Glass has touched a nerve in all of us. I haven't seen anything like this series before. I can't wait to absorb the lessons and dig into the discussions with my kids.

—Ryan O'Hara, Previous CEO The Topps Company, Shutterfly and realtor.com

In *That's What Dad's Are Made For,* Glass paints a beautiful picture of deep relationship between father and child. Whether intrinsically intertwined or completely severed, each word points to the relational connection everyone longs for with their fathers.

As a father and pastor, there is no calling higher or privilege more sacred than holding the role of "dad." Graciously, our heavenly Father shares the wonder of fatherhood with us. He is a portrayal of faithful love for us as his children to know that we belong to his family, that we may approach him without fear and always trust in his character.

This book will surely champion fathers to be faithful moment by moment to pursue their high calling, by God's grace and for his glory, and for the eternal happiness of their children.

—Brad Beggs, Pastor and Father

Smart. Playful. Fun. This book is a beautiful resource to help a child relate to his or her father at a deeper level. Parental connection is a critical component to long-term emotional stability, and this is a brilliant way to help make that connection in the most crucial years of development.

—Kirstin Carey, Certified Holistic Nutritionist

It is so incredibly vital for children to have strong role models. Adults who speak positively or negatively into a child's life make a profound difference. Boys need fathers to teach them how to be good men. Girls need fathers to teach them their value. Amanda's book is a timely reminder that we all need good fathers— biological or chosen.

—Kathleen Grehl, Sr. Mentoring Supervisor, Family Guidance

THAT'S WHAT DADS ARE MADE FOR

AMANDA B GLASS

ILLUSTRATED BY BEV JOHNSON

The Made For Books

Published by Redemption Press, PO Box 427, Enumclaw, WA 98022

Illustrated by Bev Johnson

Cover design & layout by Kevin Dinello | peculiarpxl.com

ISBN 13: 978-1-64645-155-5 (Paperback)
 978-1-64645-156-2 (ePub)
 978-1-64645-157-9 (Mobi)

Library of Congress Catalog Card Number: 2020908017

AUTHOR'S NOTE

There were many questions I had about my dad when I was growing up. Sure, he lived with me and worked hard to support our family, but for years I didn't remember sharing much quality time with him. He didn't engage in tender moments or conversations, after-school activities, or spend much time with me one on one. As a child, our relationship didn't meet my expectations, and I had few ways to express my feelings.

It wasn't until I had children of my own, then more recently after my dad passed away, that my perspective and understanding about our relationship matured. My eyes were opened to his present hand throughout my life. We would sing oldies in the car together, play card games on the living room floor, and watch talent shows on TV. No, my dad wasn't an emotional guy, but he did show his affection in simple, everyday moments.

One day, while on a family vacation, our daughter needed help getting down from jetty rocks. My husband lifted her up and placed her toes back into the sand. She blurted out, "That's what dads are made for." Not only did she get what took me so many years to see, but she inspired the idea for this book and the many "Made For" books to come.

No matter what defines a family, children are connected to their fathers. I hope that this book illuminates the connections you've already made with each other and helps you build a solid foundation for future growth. May you enjoy *That's What Dads Are Made For!*

To My Dad—You were a great father. This one's for you!

This man is my dad. But what does that mean?
Let's think about this together and work as a team.

Is my dad supposed to be this or be that?
Should he wear his hair long, or short with a hat?

Is my dad like a Santa, giving me what I want, what I wish?
Is he a tough, strong guy, or does he just want to fish?

Some dads are alike and remind me of mine.
But others seem different, and I wonder sometimes.

My grandpa is a short guy, and I see him a lot.
My neighbor has two sons, and he captains a yacht.

Greyson's dad is tall, and he cooks with pans and pots.

My uncle is a painter, and he's covered in spots.

Sal's dad over there—he sits in a chair.

Hannah's dad makes me laugh while he's cutting my hair.

I've been thinking it over a little here and a little there.
Dads aren't all the same, but they can all show they care.

My dad might be different than Hannah's or Sal's.
But that's okay because we all can be pals.

I've listed the ways my dad makes me feel special.
It helps me feel cozy, and these questions I can settle.

One time on the rocks,
I was climbing so high.
My dad reached out his hands,
and I felt safe to fly.

He caught me up high
and helped me to soar.
I tell you right now,
that's what my dad was made for!

After school when I'm watching shows on TV,
my dad crawls near and throws a blanket on me.

He tucks me in tight and lets out a roar.
I'm happy *that's what my dad was made for!*

One day at the beach, I was buried in sand.

My dad pulled me out, and I did a handstand.

He clapped his hands and yelled, "Show me more!"
I'm so proud *that's what my dad was made for!*

Sometimes when my dad and I ride in our car,
he turns on the radio during trips near or far.

He bursts into song, then he points to me.
I take it from there. We sing happy and free.

We sing a duet all the way to the store.
I'm so glad *that's what my dad was made for!*

Once we were sitting on a blanket at night, looking up at the stars, and things felt so right.

He pointed to the sky and said, "That star's bright like you.
You're important to me, and I hoped you knew."

He tells me he loves me and so much more.
And I love *that's what my dad was made for!*

My dad works at home and travels far away.
But no matter where he's sleeping, I can trust what he'll say.

He tells me hello as he walks in the door.
And once again, *that's what my dad was made for!*

place your photo here

Now let's take this a smidge further
and think a bit more.
How is your dad special?
What is your dad made for?

First, see how you two look
with your faces side by side.
Find a picture of you and your dad
and place it inside.

Next, fill in the spaces.
Let your ideas flow.
With a little thought,
they'll help you and your dad grow.

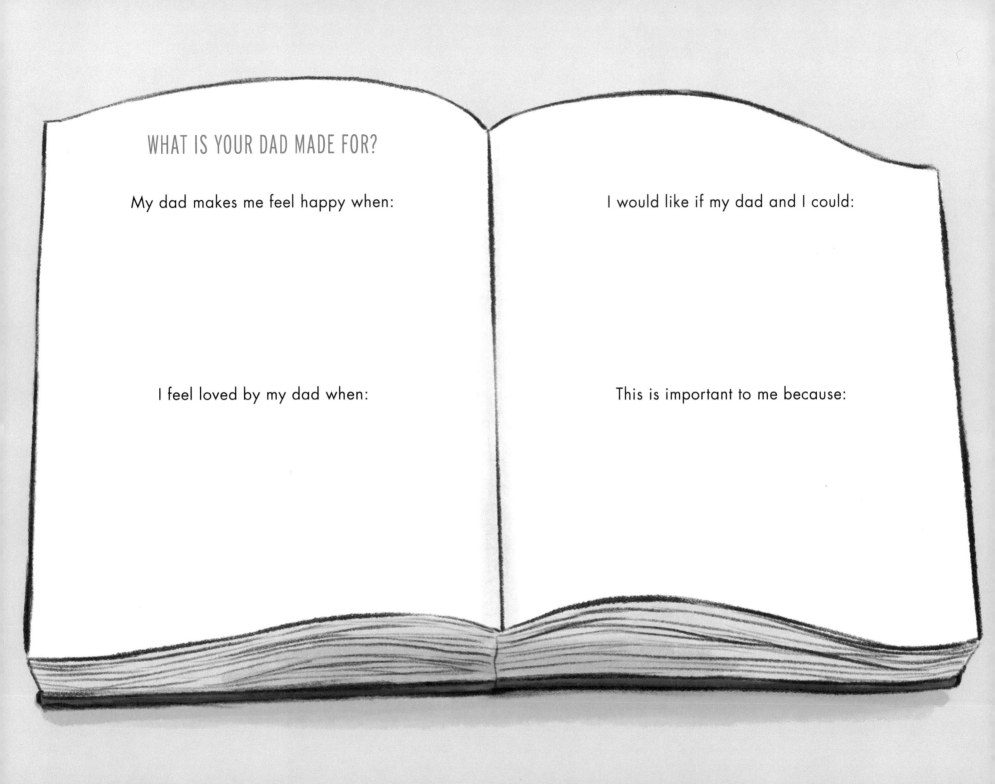

WHAT IS YOUR DAD MADE FOR?

My dad makes me feel happy when:

I feel loved by my dad when:

I would like if my dad and I could:

This is important to me because:

Your dad is special just the way that he is.
I hope you understand this after taking our quiz.

Dads aren't made perfect, not a single one.
It's important you know this as his daughter or son.

Let it sink into your heart, deep down in your core.
You're connected, and *that's what your dad was made for!*

Finally brothers and sisters, whatever is true, whatever is honorable, whatever is just, whatever is pure, whatever is lovely, whatever is commendable—if there is any moral excellence and if there is anything praiseworthy—dwell on these things.

Philippians 4:8

ORDER INFORMATION

 **The Made For Books**

To order additional copies of this book, please visit
themadeforbooks.com, amazon.com, or wherever books are sold.

CPSIA information can be obtained
at www.ICGtesting.com
Printed in the USA
LVHW020948101220
673819LV00013B/213